AUG – 2 2001

MARC BROWN

ARTHUR'S NOSE

25th Anniversary Limited Edition

Little, Brown and Company

Boston New York London

Dear Families and Friends,

Every child needs someone who believes in him or her and offers unconditional love. For me, that was my Grandma Thora. She encouraged my imagination and love of drawing. Without her Arthur would not exist.

As I tell children and adults when they ask where I get my ideas, the best things happen in real life. All of the Arthur characters really existed — I want to thank my family, teachers, and friends for inspiration. Many of the early books reflect the predicaments my own children were then dealing with in their lives. Now that Tolon, Tucker, and Eliza have outgrown Arthur and D.W., I do a lot of eavesdropping and observing, looking for issues families will find helpful in some way.

Studio

When I'm writing the Arthur books, I'm writing for children, but I also have adults in mind. I don't really think of myself as a children's book author, but rather an author of books for families.

Arthur has given me a special connection to families all over the world. And I want you to know I never take that relationship and trust for granted. Every morning when I go to work in the barn behind our house, I feel like the luckiest man alive because I'm doing what I love to do. The past twenty-five years have provided many satisfying adventures for Arthur and D.W., and I must confess, tagging along has been a terrific adventure for me as well.

Marc Brown

Pilot Hill Farm
Tisbury, Massachusetts
July 2000

Arthur's Nose Through the Years

1976

1980

1983

1987

1993

2000

Fun Facts

Arthur lives in Elwood City and is in the third grade at Lakewood Elementary School.

Arthur has a pet puppy named Pal.

Arthur's favorite TV show is *The Bionic Bunny Show*.

Muffy's real name is Mary.

The Brain's real name is Alan.

Sue Ellen is a karate expert.

Arthur has a teddy bear named Stanley.

D.W. has an imaginary friend named Nadine.

Arthur's Grandma Thora has a dog named Killer, who likes to lick people.

Muffy and Francine have the same middle name — Alice.

D.W. stands for Dora Winifred.

Prunella has an older sister named Rubella.

Binky is repeating the third grade.

Fern loves poetry.

Mr. Ratburn's desk is full of secret drawers.

Francine's greatest fear is having to wear a dress.

Arthur and his friends' favorite hangout is The Sugar Bowl.

The Brain wants to be the first person on Mars when he grows up.

Buster plays the tuba in the school orchestra.

Marc Brown in
third grade.

Arthur Read in
third grade.

The Brown family on
vacation: Mom, Marc,
Dad, Bonnie, Kimberly,
and Colleen.

The Read family on vacation:
Baby Kate, Mom, Dad, D.W.,
and Arthur.

Arthur picks out glasses with
his mother in *Arthur's Eyes*.

Alligator

Arthur and I try out new noses.

I wore glasses as a
college student.

D.W. and Arthur playing together.

Bonnie and me playing together.

Me (age five) with Santa Claus.

Francine with Santa in *Arthur's Christmas.*

My Grandma Thora and my sister Bonnie.

D.W. and Grandma Thora in *Arthur's Chicken Pox.*

My sister Bonnie is also the inspiration for Francine.

The original manuscript for *Arthur's Nose*

Arthur's Nose / By Marc Brown

4-5 { This is Arthur's house.
{ This is Arthur. He is worried about his nose.

This is Arthur's mom.
This is Arthur's dad.
6-7 { This is Arthur's sister.
This is Arthur's sister.
They all ~~like~~ love Arthur, and they all like his nose.

{ One day Arthur decided he didn't like his nose.   **Ahhchooo!**
8-9 { He had a cold and his nose was red.
{ His sister thought his nose looked funny.

{ His nose was a nuisance at school.
{ Francine who sat in front of Arthur, ~~at school~~ complained to the teacher
10-11 { that Arthur's nose was ~~bothering~~ her.   **"I want to change my seat!"**
                                      always

{ When Arthur played hide and seek,   **Snuff.**
12-13 { friends always found him first.

{ His friends thought his nose was funny.   **Snifle.**
14-15 { But what could he do about it?

16-17 { He could change his nose! That's what he could do about it!

{ Arthur told his friends that he was going to the rhinologist for a new nose.
18-19 { His friends were very surprised.   **Sniff.**

{ Doctor house was very helpful. She suggested that Arthur try on pictures
20-21 { of different noses. That way he could choose the one he liked best.
                                                          Sniff. Snuff!

{ Arthur tried on all kinds of noses.
22-23 { Chicken Fish Elephant Toucan
{ Koala Bear Hippopotamus Armadillo

{ This was going to be a difficult decision.
24-25 { Goat Mouse Rabbit Zebra
{ Alligator Rhinoceros

26-27 { Arthur's friends waited outside to see which nose he would choose.
{ "I'm going to miss Arthur's old nose."
{ "I wonder what his new nose will look like?"
{ "I wonder if we'll recognize him?"   **All quotes in bubbles**
{ "Do you think it will look better than mine?"
{ "Maybe he won't want to play with us!"
{ "I can't believe it! It's Arthur!"
{ "Wow!"
28-29 { Arthur hadn't changed his nose at all. "I tried on every nose there was. I'm just not me
{ without my nose!", said Arthur.   **It's a nice nose!**   **I still want to change my seat at school.**

30 { There's a lot more to Arthur than his nose.

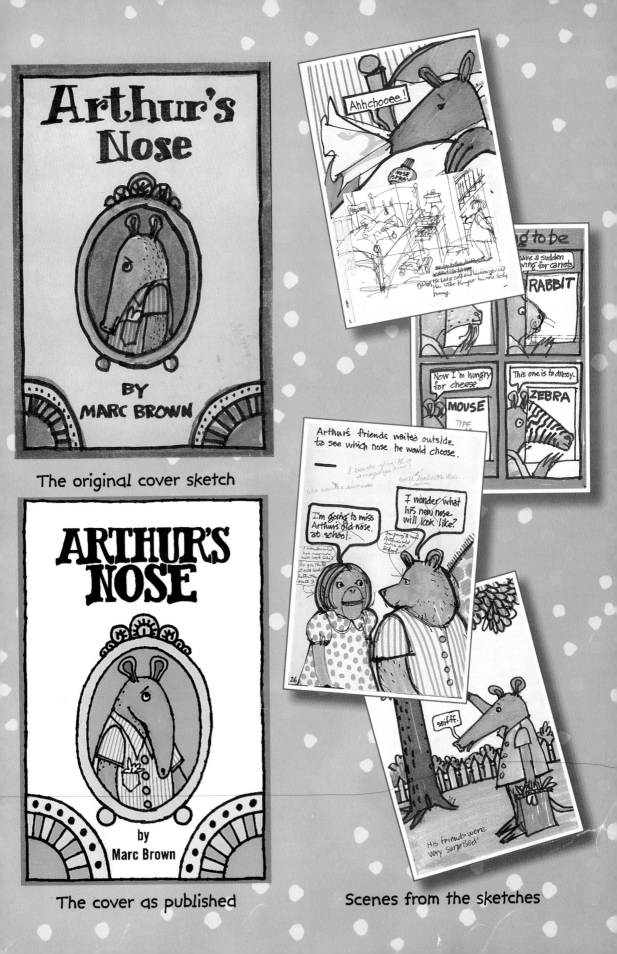

The original cover sketch

The cover as published

Scenes from the sketches

Dear Reader,

Who would have guessed twenty-five years ago that an aardvark who worried about his nose would become a children's book sensation?

When Marc Brown created Arthur in 1976, cats, dogs, and rabbits were the animal characters usually found in children's books. Now and then an occasional aardvark would appear in an alphabet book. So when *Arthur's Nose* was published by Little, Brown and Company, it was somewhat daring to expect that children would relate to the foibles of this creature. Marc Brown has not only a nose for a good story but a clever way of illustrating it; he knows what will appeal to children and how to convey childhood experiences in a humorous way to which all children can respond.

The idea for Arthur came when Marc's son Tolon requested a bedtime story with a weird animal. Thinking quickly, Marc started at the beginning of the alphabet — an aardvark named Arthur popped into his mind, and the character that would become famous was born.

The first book developed into a series of picture books called Arthur Adventures, and the antics of this captivating aardvark were off and running. Arthur has become "everychild," facing the dilemmas that arise with family, school, and friends. Whether the worries are a scary teacher, a new sibling, or having to wear glasses, they resonate with children who are trying to sort out similar predicaments. By sharing Arthur's problems, kids respond to his experiences and ways of problem solving in everyday challenges. Marc says: "The most interesting and funniest things happen in real life." He has captured them perfectly and humorously in the dozens of Arthur books he has written.

Public libraries can attest to Arthur's popularity. Simply put, the books fly off the shelves! As soon as new ones arrive, eager hands are reaching for them. When one young fan came to the library for storytime every week, he would rush up to the poster of Arthur in the Children's Room and declare, "I love you, Arthur!" Another loyal fan joined the library's summer reading club. Each day he came to report on the book that he had read to earn his credit, and each day it was the same Arthur book. It took weeks for the Children's Librarian to convince him to try other stories, and he finally complied — by reading another book about Arthur!

Parents and children alike are fans of the books, proof that Arthur's appeal is ageless. From looking klutzy at playing ball, to a family vacation that turns into a disaster, to having a secret admirer, Arthur's adventures satisfy our sense of humor and poetic justice. From one book to the next, Arthur is always in top form, providing chuckles and grins, befriending children, and speaking to their daily ups and downs.

Here's to Arthur and his creator, Marc Brown. Cheers and applause in celebration of the twenty-fifth anniversary of the first Arthur book. We want you to remain eight years old forever (which Marc has promised will happen) and to stay as charming, delightful, and wise as you have been all these years.

Just think, it all began with a nose. Arthur, you have brought and continue to bring millions of smiles to readers' faces. As the first book says: "There's a lot more to Arthur than his nose." Indeed, there is. Your fans know.

Julie Cummins
Coordinator, Children's Services
The New York Public Library

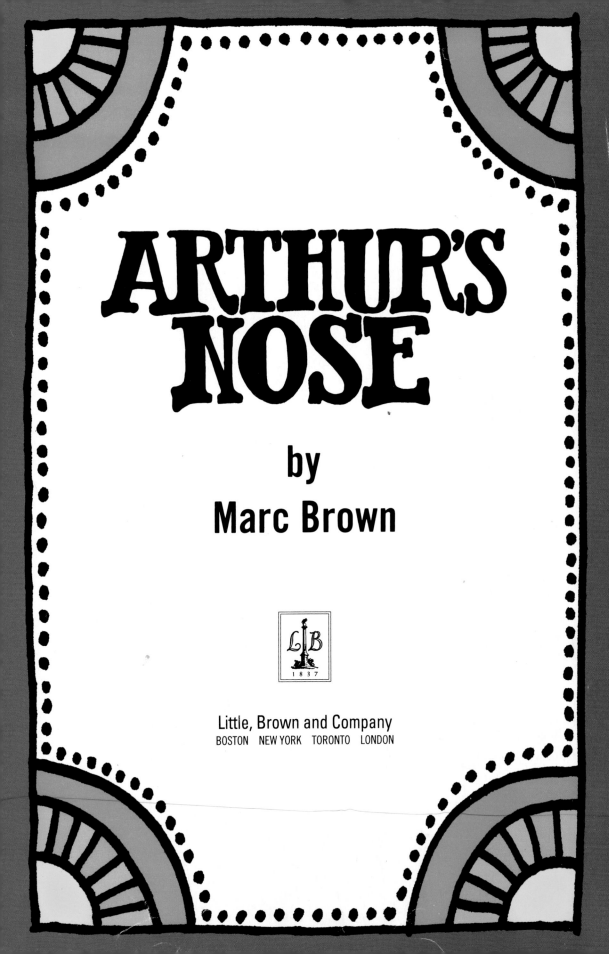

ARTHUR'S NOSE

by
Marc Brown

Little, Brown and Company
BOSTON NEW YORK TORONTO LONDON

ISBN 0-316-11884-2
Library of Congress Control Number 00-106832

10 9 8 7 6 5 4 3 2 1

WOR

Printed in the United States of America

This is Arthur's house.

This is Arthur.
He is worried
about his nose.

This is Arthur's mom.

This is Arthur's dad.

This is Arthur's sister.

They all love Arthur, and they all like his nose.

One day Arthur decided he didn't like his nose.
He had a cold and his nose was red.
His sister thought his nose looked funny.

His nose was a nuisance at school.
Francine, who sat in front of Arthur, complained to the teacher that Arthur's nose was always bothering her.

When Arthur played hide-and-seek,
friends always found him first.

His friends thought his nose was funny.
But what could he do about it?

He could change his nose!
That's what he could
do about it.

Arthur told his friends that he was going
to the rhinologist for a new nose.
His friends were very surprised.

Doctor Louise was very helpful. She suggested that Arthur try on pictures of different noses. That way he could choose the one he liked best.

Arthur tried on all kinds of noses.

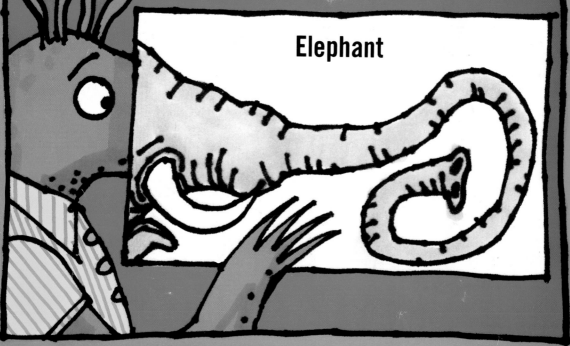

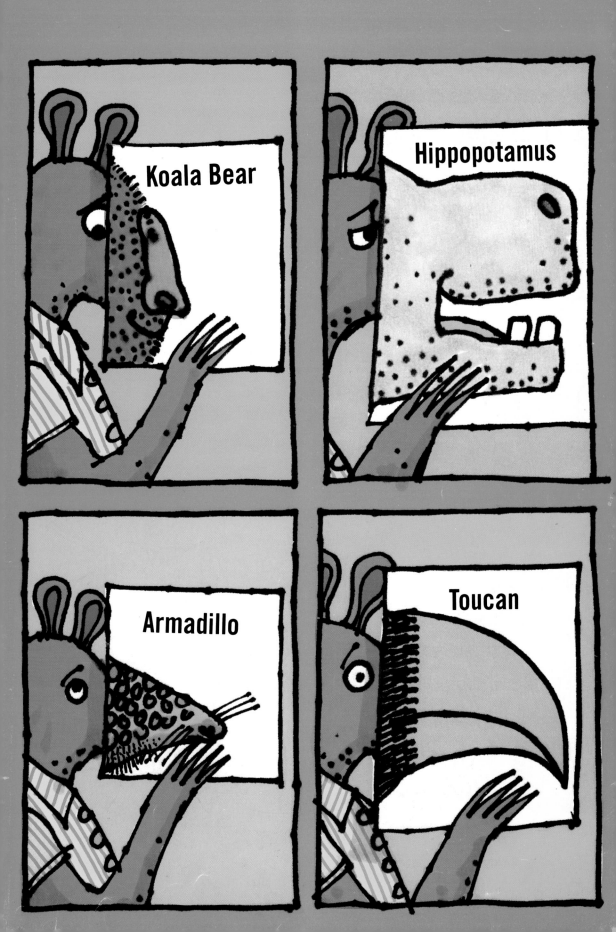

This was going to be a difficult decision.

Arthur hadn't changed his nose at all.

"I tried on every nose there was.
I'm just not me without my nose!"
said Arthur.

It's a nice nose.

There's a lot more to Arthur than his nose.